COMIC PANEL
FIST AWARDS
2 0 1 7
WINNER
BEST COMIC
ARTIST

COMIC PANEL
FIST AWARDS
2 0 1 7
WINNER
BEST
COLOURIST

COMIC PANEL
FIST AWARDS
2 0 1 8
WINNER
BEST
PACKAGED
COMIC

COMIC PANEL
FIST AWARDS
2 0 1 8
WINNER
BEST
COLOURIST

COMIC PANEL
FIST AWARDS
2 0 1 8
WINNER
BEST COMIC
ARTIST

AEGIS

CREATED BY

MARTIN OKONKWO AND EMMANUEL EZEABIAMA

VOLUME 1

LINE ART / LETTERS
MARTIN OKONKWO

COVERS
GODWIN AKPAN

MARTIN OKONKWO

JEFF OYEM

COLOURS
ETUBI ONUCHEYO

TARELLA PABLO

EBERE JOSIAH

MARTIN OKONKWO

SCRIPTS
CHIKA EZEABIAMA

J.C NOVA

EDITORS
ZUBERU KADIRI

OKEOGHENE OVUOMAGHE

CHIMA EZEIBE

PROJECT MANAGERS
PATRICK IJITI

DEYO ADEBIYI

OGOO EZEOLU

EXEC PRODUCER
MARTIN OKONKWO

SPECIAL THANKS TO
DAVID OGBUELI,

OKECHUKWU EZE CHIMA EZEIBE,

OGOO OKONKWO,

LINEGUAGE STUDIOS

epoch JUL 2019 ALL RIGHTS RESERVED f EPOCHCOMICS @EPOCHCOMICS_NG @EPOCHSTUDIOSNG

THERE ARE **THREE** COSMIC REGIONS

THE **EMPYREA:** FAR BEYOND THE COSMOS...ALSO CALLED THE **NORTH CITY**

THE **ECHOSTRUM:** HOME TO THE STARS, **GALAXIES** AND PLANETS

THE **ATMOS**, COMPRISING THE SKIES AND **CLOUDS**

AND BENEATH THEM ALL, THERE IS THE **EARTH....** HOME OF THE **DWELLERS.**

THIS IS LAGOS, NIGERIA

THE EXTRA-DIMENSIONAL *INFLUENCES* THE REALM OF THE DWELLERS. THE THINGS THAT THE DWELLERS CALL *ACCIDENTS*, LUCK AND CHANCE ARE PURELY *ORCHESTRATED* BY THE AGENTS.

IT'S A *BATTLE* AND THERE IS NO *MIDDLE GROUND*, ALL DWELLERS ARE YIELDED TO *EITHER* SIDE.

DEDE PHILIPS IS IGNORANT OF THESE *FACTS* AND HAS *CONSEQUENTLY* LANDED ON A TOUGH SPOT.

THRONE

03.

I LOVE YOU SO MUCH...
THOSE WERE HER VERY LAST WORDS...
BOOOMSH
BOOOMSSSH
HE HEARD GUNSHOTS, THEN TYRES SCREECHING. HE DARTED OUT OF THE OFFICE
ANGELA! ANGELA !!!
WITH HIS FRIEND, FEMI OSHODI TRAILING BEHIND

06-

DO IT!

YES! PULL THE TRIGGER

A SPLIT SECOND LATER

QUICK **AZARA** JAM THE GUN AND EXPEL THE **IMPS**, I WILL TAKE ON THE **WARRING PRETOR**.

WE MUST **PROTECT** HIM BECAUSE THE **OVERLORD** NEEDS HIM AND NIKKY NEEDS HIM ALIVE....HENCE SHE **SUMMONED US.**

AFFIRMED **KABZA!**

07.

WHEN ALL *DWELLERS* ARE IN OUR CLUTCHES , WE WILL CONTROL BOTH THE *ATMOS* AND THE *ECHOSTRUM* AND ALL YOU SERAPHS WILL BE OUT OF *JOBS* FOREVER! HA HA HA HA!!!

THE SOVEREIGN PLAN OF THE *OVERLORD* IS IN MOTION ALREADY AND THERE'S *NOTHING* YOUR MASTER CAN DO ABOUT IT. THE *DWELLERS* WILL RULE THEIR SPHERE FOREVER...

AT THE *RATE* THE DWELLERS ARE GOING.... YOUR MASTER'S PIPE DREAM IS A *HOAX!* HA HA HA HA!!!

HOW *DARE* YOU SPEAK ABOUT THE *OVERLORD* LIKE THAT!

ARRGGHHH!!! THE *BLINDING* LIGHT SWORD!

10.

RETURN TO THE ECHOSTRUM YOU LOATHSOME PRETOR.

GHHAAH

AAAIiEEE

DADDY!!!

NIKKY! WHAT IS IT, SWEETHEART?

SCARY LOOKING PEOPLE...THEY WERE TRYING TO HURT YOU, BUT TWO GIANTS CAME AND SAVED YOU

I SAW THEM IN MY DREAMS, THEY KEPT COMING ---PLEASE DON'T LEAVE ME DADDY.

I LOVE YOU DAD.....I NEED YOU AROUND

I'M HERE, SWEETIE, AND WILL ALWAYS BE--- NOTHING IS GOING TO HAPPEN TO YOU.

MARINA, LAGOS ISLAND

EAGLE PRESS TOWERS TWO DAYS LATER

WELCOME BACK TO WORK, DEDE. WE **MISSED** YOU; WE WILL GO THROUGH THIS AS A FAMILY.

I **APPRECIATE**, FEMI. I THINK I'LL BE ALRIGHT ONCE I GET **WORKING** AGAIN

WOW! GOOD TO SEE YOU **DEDE!**

THANKS, ADEOLA.

YOU'RE STILL **YET** TO GIVE ME THE **DETAILS** ABOUT ABUJA

I **DON'T** WANT TO TALK ABOUT THAT FOR NOW

13

SHORTLY
LATER

JUST PUT IT IN THE ABLE *HANDS* OF THE *MAKER* HE WILL HELP YOU *HEAL*, IT IS WELL MY FRIEND

DEDE, I KNOW WE CAN'T FILL THE *VOID* IN YOUR HEART, BUT ITS GOOD TO HAVE YOU *BACK*

THANK YOU SIR

THE VILLA, ABUJA SAME TIME

OH *PLEASE!* WHERE WAS HE WHEN THEY *KILLED* MY WIFE

DIKKO PAYNE'S OFFICE

MORNING SIR! WE JUST GOT A CALL THAT HE HAS RETURNED TO WORK, WHAT DO WE DO NOW?

THE INSIDE MAN *WANTS* MORE *TIME.* DO WE WAIT?

JUST TWO *SIMPLE* STEPS, RETRIEVE THE *FLASH DRIVE* AND GET RID OF HIM. ABI ANY *WAHALA?*

TEAGLE PRESS TOWERS, SAME NIGHT

NO TIME MY FRIEND! WE MUST ACT *QUICKLY* DO IT TONIGHT AND MAKE SURE WE GET IT. NO *SLACKING* THIS TIME. THE LORDS IS TOO BIG FOR ONE *DWELLER* TO BE A *THREAT* TO US.

15

DEDE WORKS LATE INTO THE NIGHT
CLICK CLICK
I STILL CAN'T FIGURE OUT EXACTLY WHAT TO DO WITH IT
THIS VIDEO IS JUST ATROCIOUS
PART OF ME INSISTS ON HOLDING ON TO IT
FOR A GOOD REASON TOO. IT CAN BRING THEM ALL DOWN
bee -beep
HAND THE FLASHDRIVE OVER RIGHT NOW. GIVE ME THE BAG!
THEIR ILLS MUST BE EXPOSED ---
OH GREAT.

BLAM BLAM

SKREEEEEEEEEEEECCCHH

WHAT ON *EARTH...* ?

WHAM

EEEEEEEEEEEEEECCCHH

THE BAG, *NOW!*

UGH?

LEAVE HIM ALONE YOU TWO!

MIND YOUR *BUSINESS* OLD MAN.

17

OGA JANITOR? AT THIS TIME?

I SAID, LET HIM GO!

BLAM BANG

NOW, YOU STUBBORN FOOL.... EH?

NIKKY! I HAVE TO GET TO HER

GET HIM!

I DON'T THINK SO

GRROOWWL

KUSU AND PIAKA, I KNEW YOU BOTH HAD TO BE BEHIND THIS

WELL....THIS IS A FAIR FIGHT NOW!

18

I AM SALVEZZA, CHAMPION OF THE ORDER OF SERAPHS
I CAN SEE YOU BROUGHT ALONG YOUR ENTIRE REGIMENT
NOW, WILL YOU LEAVE IN PEACE OR BY FORCE ?
SERAPH! THIS IS NO BUSINESS OF YOURS
WE ARE GOING NO WHERE UNTIL HE IS DESTROYED!
"CHUCKLE" VERY WELL THEN...
SHKK
LET'S SEE HOW YOU HOLD OUT AGAINST THESE TOOLS OF ENLIGHTENMENT
SHKK
FREE RETURN PASS TO THE UNDERWORLD ANYONE?
GHRROOWWWWLLL

Dede's Residence : same night
NO!
JUST WHEN I THOUGHT IT COULDN'T GET ANY WORSE
AMAKA! EH...EH...EH? WHERE IS NIKKY?!
AHH! OGA DEM CARRI GUN, DEM BEAT ME, NEARLY KILL ME, JAM MY HEAD FOR WALL, I COME COLLAPSE. WEN I WAKE UP AS YOU ENTER I NO SEE NIKKY. DEM KIDNAP AM?!
IF U WANT HER BACK YOU KNOW WHAT WE WANT
NIKKY! WHAT HAVE I DONE?!
SECOND DEATH

STILL KEEPING DETAILS OF THE POST-VILLA EVENTS FROM ME? ...EVEN THE POLICE THINK YOU'RE HIDING SOMETHING.

WHAT'S GOING ON BUDDIE? TALK TO ME. I'D LIKE TO HELP

TRUST ME, YOU CAN'T. TRUTH IS, I'M NOT EVEN SURE I UNDERSTAND WHAT'S GOING ON ANYMORE

ALL HELL HAS BROKEN LOOSE IN MY LIFE, AND I DON'T WANT TO DRAG YOU INTO ALL THE MESS

...THE FOURTH DIMENSION

HALT, MOWU!!!

KABZA! THE REPROBATE SOUL WHOM YOU GUARD MUST EMBRACE HIS FATE- IT IS SEALED THIS VERY DAY! LEGION, ADVANCE!!!

06.

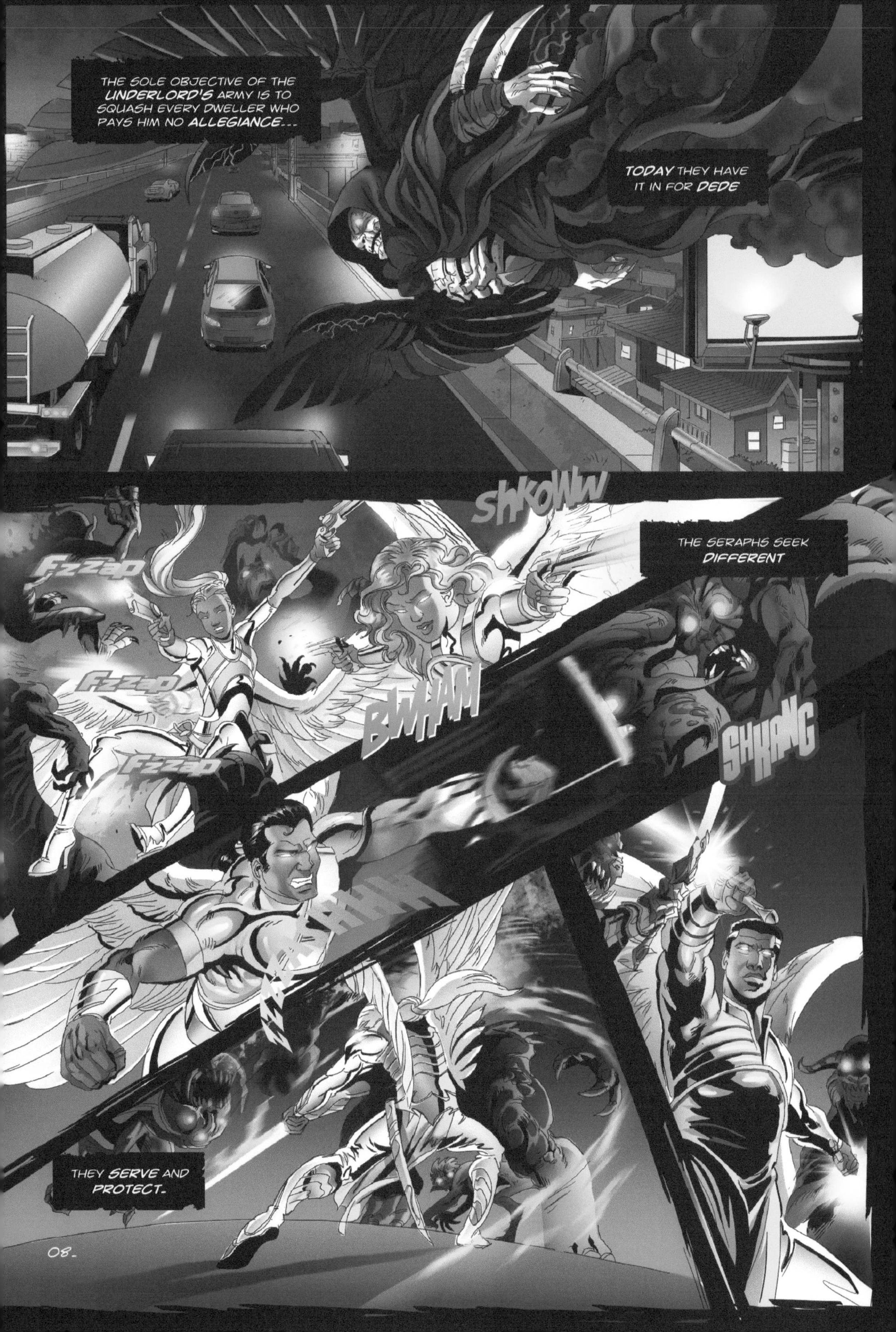

THE SOLE OBJECTIVE OF THE **UNDERLORD'S** ARMY IS TO SQUASH EVERY DWELLER WHO PAYS HIM NO **ALLEGIANCE...**

TODAY THEY HAVE IT IN FOR **DEDE**

SHKOWW

THE SERAPHS SEEK **DIFFERENT**

FZZap

FZZap

BWHAM

FZZap

SHKANG

THEY **SERVE** AND **PROTECT.**

08.

CLOTHE THEM IN *DARKNESS*, LET THEIR FEAR BE THEIR *END* AND LET THEIR END BE THEIR *DOOM*

TWO *BEINGS* OF LIGHT BURST THROUGH THE *DARK* CLOUDS

RIGHT AWAY! THOSE *GHOULS* ARE GONERS!

SALVEZZA

WARRIOR, UNDO THE *SPAWNS*! MOWU STINGS NO DWELLER!

ZADKA

ONE *DOWN*, ONE TO....?

FRAAXX

GHHHRRHH

09.

THESE WORTHLESS NYMPHS ARE NEVER-DO-WELLERS YOU CAN'T SAVE THEM
THEY MAY NEVER APPRECIATE IT, BUT WE FIGHT FOR HOPE
MOWU, THERE IS NO VICTORY FOR YOU HERE, BE GONE.
NOT GOOD!
THE MIND OF A WEAK AND IGNORANT DWELLER IS EASY PREY FOR PRETORS
...THE SUSCEPTIBLE TRUCKER IS TAKEN OVER AND MANIPULATED
HONK!!!
JUST ONE MOMENT OF CONFUSION...

AND...
WH ...WHAT'S HAPPENING, KENE!!?
KRASH
KRRRASSSSH
NO! I CAN'T DIE THIS WAY...OH MY...HELP!
OUT OF DESPERATION, DEDE UTTERS HIS FIRST TRUE PLEA FOR HELP
SHVATANGG
GOOD CHOICE OF WORDS, FRIEND. GRANTED!
BASH
ba-WOom

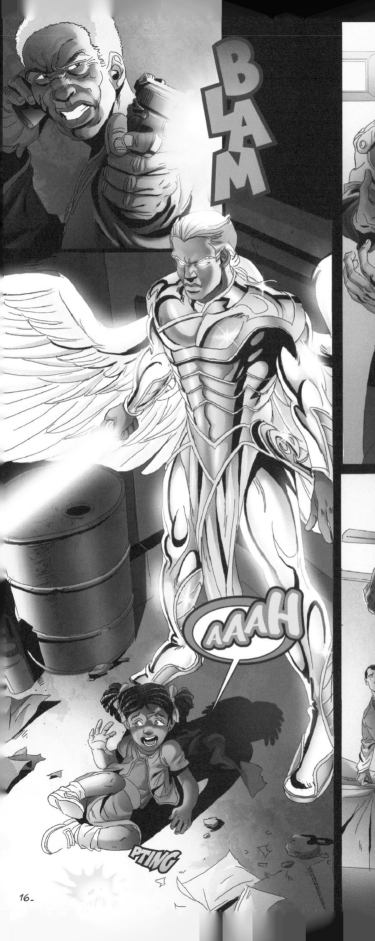

16.

Pa Adebanjo's Residence
Same night

17.

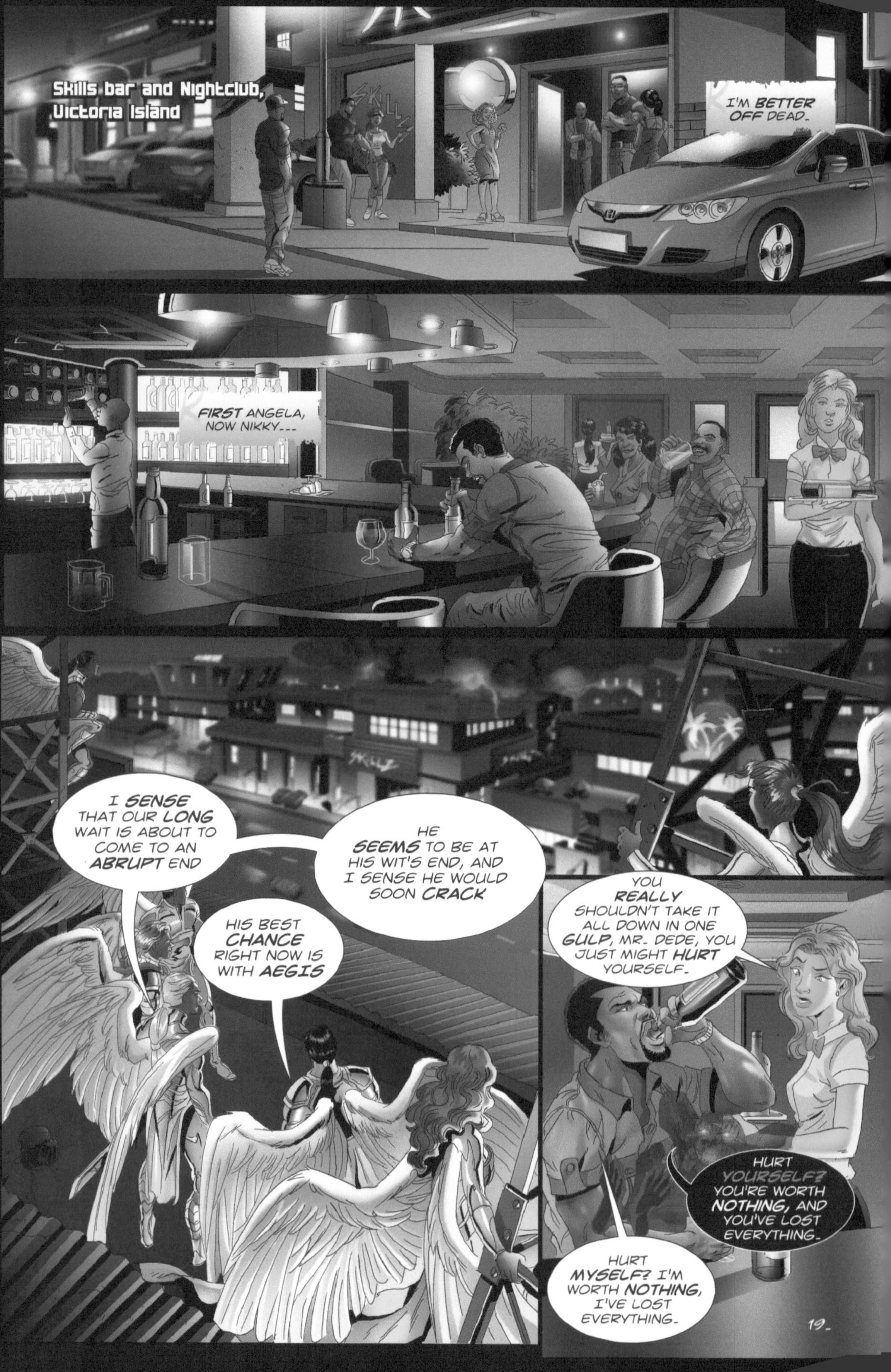

20.

THERE IS ONLY THE DARKNESS.
GROAN
...THE WEAKNESS
...MADDENING PAIN
THUD!
AND THE EVER-GROWING SENSE...
SSSSSSSS...
THAT SOMETHING IS AMISS!
SSSSS...

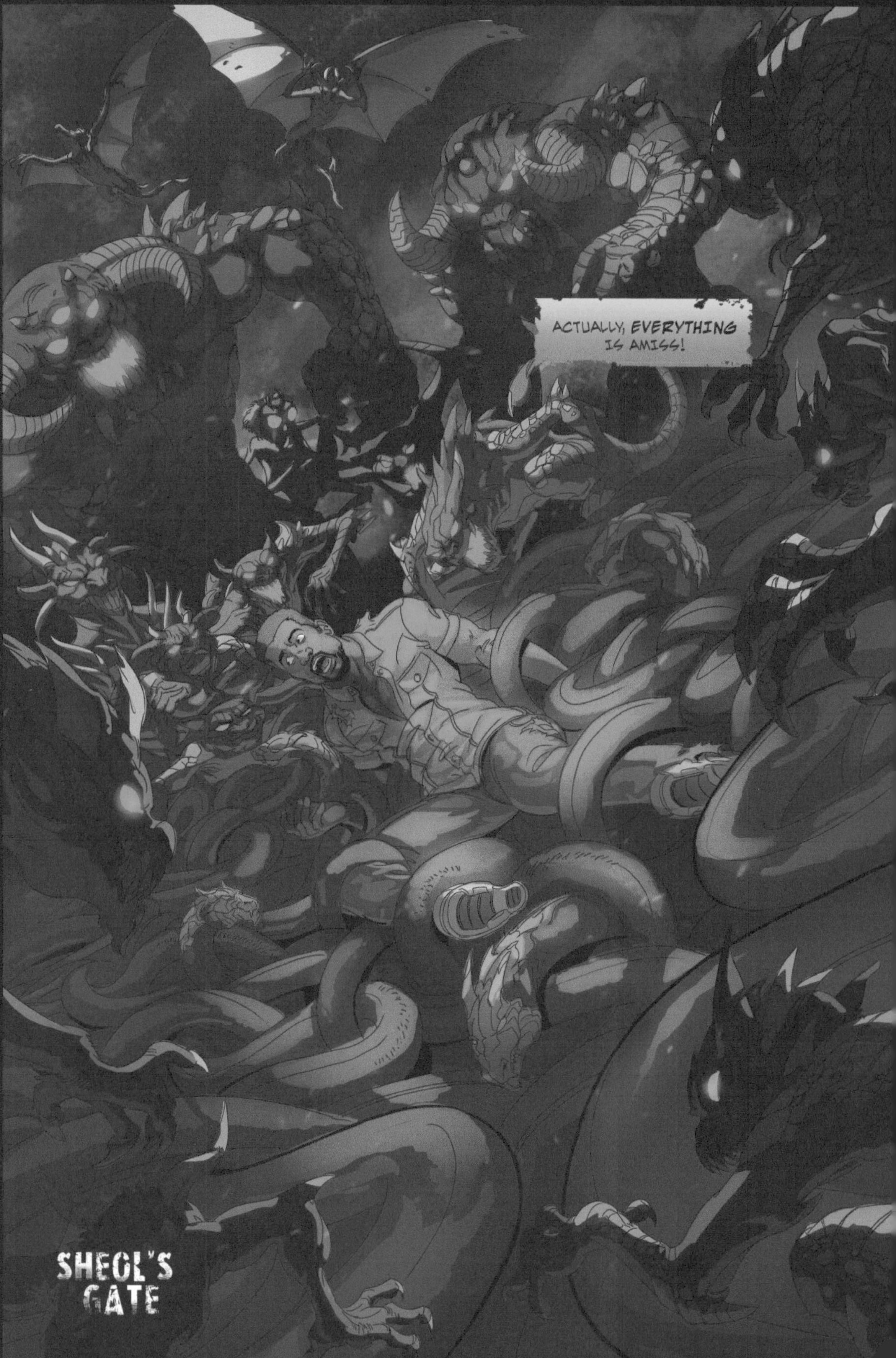
ACTUALLY, EVERYTHING IS AMISS!
SHEOL'S GATE

THE DARKNESS QUICKLY GIVES WAY TO MADNESS.
WHAT THE HECK IS GOING ON?
THERE WAS THE DESPAIR, THEN THERE WAS THE BAR AND THE ENDLESS DRINKS.
DWELLER!!! WHY DO YOU RUN FROM YOUR WELCOME?!
WH-WHERE AM I?
THERE WAS ALSO THE DESIRE FOR SUICIDE TO END THE SUFFERING.
ARE YOU NOT GLAD TO BE HERE?
YOU, MY FRIEND, ARE AT THE GRAND RECEPTION OF THE DAMNED!
GOD! WHAT IS HAPPENING TO ME? WHAT IS GOING ON?
DON'T TELL ME YOU DON'T KNOW WHERE YOU ARE.

MY NAME IS KNIFE.

PLEASED TO MEET YOU, ER, KNIFE. HOWEVER, I HAVE A FIGHT IN 30 MINUTES.

I HAVE NO IDEA WHY YOU ARE HERE BUT...

OH, THAT'S EASY. I WAS JUST IN THE NEIGHBOURHOOD AND THOUGHT I SHOULD DROP BY...

AS SAMSON WATCHES THE INTRUDER, HE CANNOT MAKE UP HIS MIND ABOUT WHICH IS STRANGER; HOW THIS MAN GAINED ENTRY, PAST ALL THE GUARDS

FOR SAMSON, THIS IS NOT THE TIME FOR CLOWNING.

- OR HIS NAME.

I'LL KILL YOU, SEE A MOVIE - AND THEN I CAN RELAX FOR TODAY.

IF HIS FACE WASN'T SO STRAIGHT, YOU WOULD ALMOST THINK HE WAS JOKING...

AND HOW DO YOU INTEND TO DO THAT... ASSASSIN?

WELL. GOOD OLD FISTS.

...BUT ONE LOOK IN THOSE UNWAVERING EYES AND YOU COULD TELL THIS STRANGER WAS FOR REAL

THIS STRANGER WAS HERE TO KILL

AND WHAT IS THIS ABOUT?

SAMSON HAS BEEN HERE MANY TIMES. HE IS A MASTER OF THIS DANCE.
EEEEE!
SMASH
HIS TECHNIQUES, FLAWLESS, AS HE GAUGES KNIFE'S REACTION
HIS ATTACKS, EXECUTED WITH RUTHLESS PRECISION
AND WHAT IS EVIDENT IN THIS TANGO OF DEATH IS THAT HIS OPPONENT IS ALSO A MASTER
SAH!
HAHH!
BUT HE HAS SEEN ENOUGH MASTERS TO KNOW...
THAT EVEN MASTERS...
TAK
CAN BLEED!
CRASH

GROAN

GET UP! I'M JUST GETTING STARTED!

BY THE TIME THE POLICE ARRIVE, THERE WON'T BE MUCH OF YOU LEFT TO TAKE TO JAIL!

INTERESTING. HOWEVER, CONNECTING ONCE OUT OF SEVEN ATTACKS IS POOR ...

SAH!

HE SEEMS TO BE MOVING FASTER AND MORE SMOOTHLY THAN BEFORE.

I ONLY ATTACK MY OPPONENTS ONCE.

COME!

THERE IS NO PAUSE OR HESITATION FROM SAMSON, THOUGH HE REALISES THEY ARE BOTH FIGHTING FOR THEIR LIVES.

AND FOR ONE OF THEM, VERY SOON...

CLEARLY, THIS IS THE DOMAIN OF THE DAMNED AND THE FINAL "RESTING PLACE" OF LOST SOULS.
THE TRUTH IS, THERE IS NO RESTING AT ALL TO BE DONE IN THIS PLACE, EXCEPT ONE CAN FIND AN EASE IN TORMENT THAT CONTINUES INTO 'FOREVER'...
AND THEN SOME...
I TRUST YOU LIKE THE VIEW; THE PLEASING REDNESS OF THE SKIES, THE WONDERFUL SCENT OF SULPHUR,
LET ME GO PLEASE!!!!
...AND THE SOOTHING SCREAMS OF TORTURE!
AH! I WOULD NOT DO THAT FOR THE WORLD, DWELLER!
WHY? WHAT HAVE I DONE?
WHAT ELSE IS AS PLEASURABLE AS SEEING ONE OF YOUR MEASLY KIND DROWNING, FOREVER, IN A POOL OF PURE BUBBLING LAVA!
OH, NOTHING. I JUST HATE YOUR KIND!

SUDDENLY, AND FROM LITERALLY NOWHERE, SOMEONE ELSE MAKES AN ENTRANCE.
I AM HERE FOR DEDE.
ZZAP
I AM AISHA AND LIKE I SAID, I AM NOT LEAVING WITHOUT THE MAN
WHO ARE YOU? AND HOW DID YOU COME HERE?
I SAID, HOW DID YOU GET HERE?
SOME OF US CAN STAND IN THAT GAP BETWEEN THE LIVING AND THE DEAD...
BETWEEN WHAT IS SEEN AND WHAT IS UNSEEN.
IN THIS PLACE, YOU HAVE NO POWER!
AND IN THIS PLACE, YOU REMAIN A LIAR!
PUNY WOMAN! I WILL PURIFY YOU WITH THE FIRE OF HELL!

JUST WHEN I THOUGHT IT COULDN'T GET ANY CRAZIER, SOMEONE NEW STEPS INTO THIS FRAY OF MADNESS!
CAN'T HELP WONDERING WHO THE TOUGH TALKING NEWCOMER IS. SHE LOOKS LIKE A NICE PERSON. WE MIGHT MEET AGAIN SOMEDAY
UNDER FAIRLY DIFFERENT CIRCUMSTANCES. POSSIBLY
BOTTOM LINE IS, EVERYONE IS DISTRACTED - AND RIGHT NOW, THAT IS NOT SUCH A BAD THING.
HOWEVER, BUT TODAY IS NOT THAT DAY!
SMART MAN.
I GUESS THE LAST THING HE IS THINKING ABOUT IS THE MOST IMPORTANT PART.
SNARL!!!
HOW THE HELL DO YOU GET OUT OF HELL?!

COME ON!
SHE IS NO ORDINARY LADY.
THIS ONE IS A WARRIOR - AND SHE IS NOT AFRAID TO MOUNT A RESISTANCE AGAINST PRETOR WARRIORS.
AND WHEN SHE RESISTS THE EVIL ONE..
THEY FLEE!
THE RUNNER IS STILL RUNNING, AWAY FROM THE COMMOTION, AWAY FROM DEMONS THAT PLAGUE HIM...
DEDE. YOU NEED TO STOP RUNNING.
BUT IN THIS PLACE, THERE IS NO DISTANCE.
LADY, I DON'T KNOW WHO YOU ARE, WHAT YOU ARE OR WHERE YOU ARE FROM. BUT IF YOU CAN, PLEASE....
HELP ME.
THAT IS WHY I AM HERE DEDE. I AM HERE TO HELP YOU. BUT YOU WILL HAVE TO...

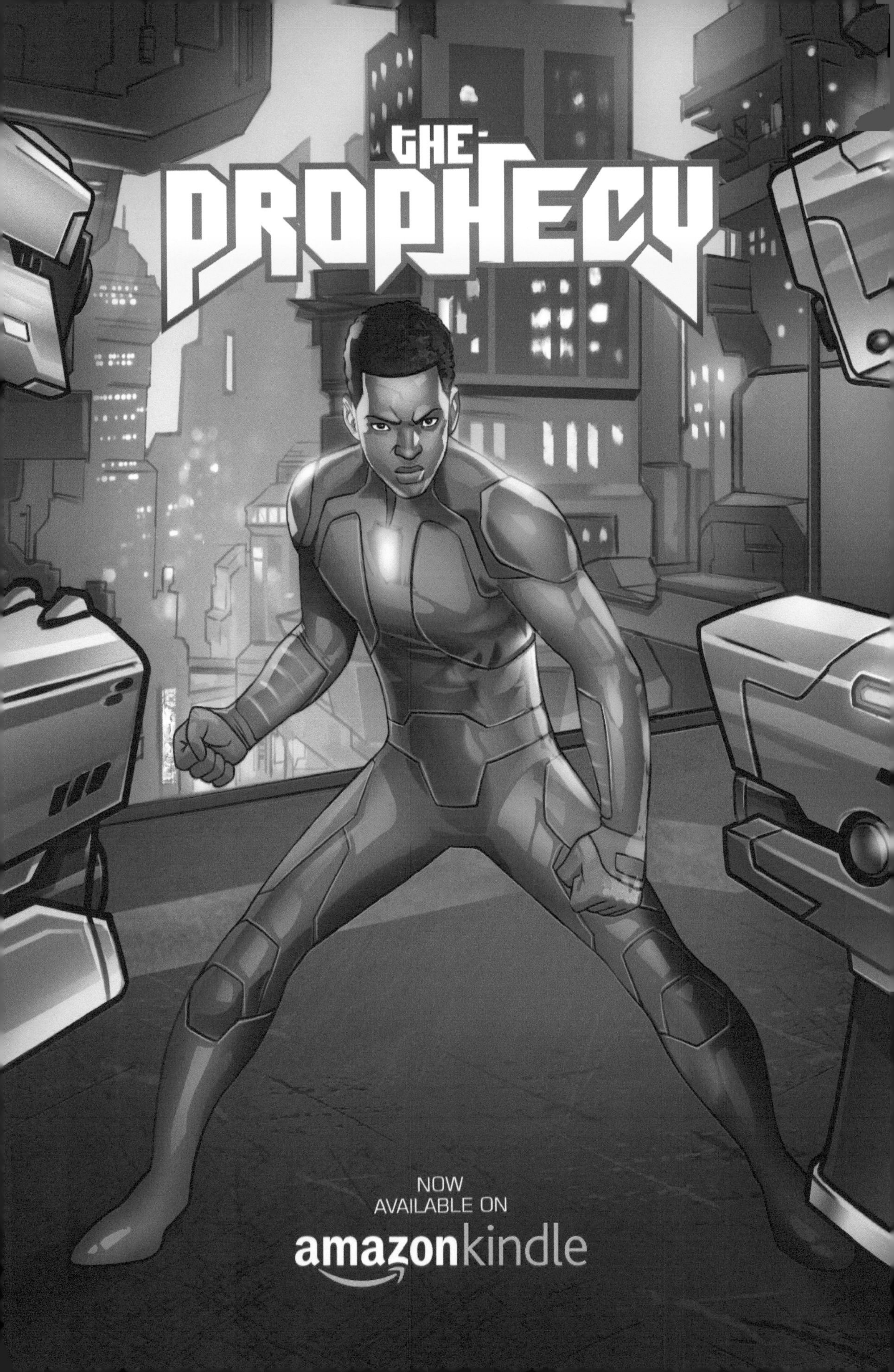

THE PROPHECY
NOW
AVAILABLE ON
amazonkindle

THE *LAST* THING ON *FEMI'S* MIND IS THAT HIS *FRIEND,* DEDE, MIGHT BE *DEAD* BECAUSE OF WHAT HE *HOLDS* IN HIS HANDS.

OR THAT HIS FRIEND'S *WIFE* IS DEAD *BECAUSE* OF IT. OR THAT HIS FRIEND'S *DAUGHTER* IS ALSO *KIDNAPPED,* BECAUSE OF IT

HE IS *SURE* HE WILL.

MONEY IS ON HIS MIND. FIFTY MILLION NAIRA IS WHAT HAS BEEN PROMISED. BUT WHAT HE HOLDS IN HIS HANDS WILL GIVE HIM ONLY A PORTION OF IT - TILL HE GETS THE OTHER PART.

THE *CHALLENGE* WITH *BETRAYALS,* HOWEVER, IS THAT THEY *DON'T* GO SO WELL IN THE END!

HERE IS THE *DRIVE.* I HAVE DONE MY PART.

INDEED

IRONIC. JUDAS ALSO BETRAYED HIS FRIEND FOR THIRTY PIECES OF SILVER.

.....!

WHAAAT !!!!?

THE INITIAL PAYMENT. *THIRTY MILLION* NAIRA, WOULD SUFFICE FOR NOW

ARRGH!

WHACK!

EXTRICATION

THE BATTLE IS ALREADY OVER.
CHECKMATE!
I FIRED THOSE FROM EARLIER. LOOKS LIKE THEY JUST "CAUGHT UP" WITH YOU...LIKE SINS.
THESE ARE NOT ORDINARY ARROWS. THESE ONES ...
KRA-BOOM
...EXPLODE!
NOW, WHAT AM I GOING TO DO WITH THESE ONES?

YASH-EN

RIGHT *UNDER* THEIR NOSES. ITS EFFECT WILL *PLAY* OUT SHORTLY.

THE *BATTLE* IS OVER, BUT THE *CAPTORS* HAVE *NO* IDEA THAT A BATTLE HAS BEEN FOUGHT, AND THAT THE *BATTLE* HAS BEEN LOST

PFFFT PFFFT PFFFT

IT TAKES ABOUT A *MINUTE,*

BUT IN THE END, THE *CAPTORS* GIVE WAY TO SLUMBER AND *SWEET* DREAMS.

EPH-PHATHA!

THE *CAPTIVE* IS *FREE* TO LEAVE, IT APPEARS.

HERE IS MY ANSWER!
OH MY GOD! OH MY GOD! HE HAS A GUN!
AH! AH! PLEAS--
A PART OF HIS SOUL IS WEARY FROM ALL THE RUNNING. A PART OF HIM WANTS TO WAIT FOR THE GUNMAN TO TURN ON HIM AND KILL HIM.
END HIS LIFE, END HIS MISERY. IT WOULD BE AN END FOR THE SADNESS THAT DROWNS HIS SOUL
AN END FROM RUNNING FROM THOSE WHO ARE CHASING HIM
pFFT!!!
pFFT!!!
pFFT!!!
AND END TO THE NEVER-ENDING CHAOS
ON THE OTHER HAND...
HE REALLY WANTS TO LIVE!
pFFT!!!
pFFT!!!
AARGH!!
ON THE OTHER HAND, HE REALLY WANTS TO FIGHT!!!

pFFT!!!
AAARRRGGGHHH
NOW, WHAT ARE MY OPTIONS?
GOTCHYA! 'LEST YOU DASH YOUR FEET AGAINST A STONE'!
HANG ON DEDE.
I'M SURE YOU HAVE A LOT OF QUESTIONS, BUT FIRST, I NEED TO EXPLAIN TO YOU WHY YOUR WIFE DIED!
I DON'T EVEN KNOW THIS GUY, BUT WHAT ARE MY OPTIONS RIGHT NOW?

THE BRIEF WAS EASY AND TO THE POINT
FIND THE MAN. RETRIEVE THE FLASH DRIVE AND A LEDGER OR INFORMATION ABOUT THEIR WHEREABOUTS...
KILL THE MAN
WITH OVER THIRTY CONFIRMED KILLS IN THE BUSINESS, THE BRIEF WAS SIMPLE ENOUGH...
HE DID NOT ENVISAGE THE BROKEN NOSE
KRASH!!!
ARRGH!
THE MISSING TEETH. HURTING NETHER REGIONS
OR HIS PREY FLYING AWAY... LITERALLY!
WHO GOES THERE?!!
AND NOT BECAUSE HE HAS LOST HIS EDGE!

THERE IS TROUBLE... THE GIRL GOT AWAY!
WHAT?! HOW?!
I'M AFRAID! WORD ON THE STREET IS THAT OGA DIKKO WANTS TO KILL US - AND THEN HE WILL GO FOR OUR FAMILIES.
LET HIM COME...
WE HAVE NO FAMILIES!
BRAVE WORDS!
WHO ARE YOU? HOW DID YOU GET IN HERE? WHAT DO YOU WANT?
HOW EPIC!
MY NAME IS KNIFE. I GET AROUND AND TO YOUR FINAL QUESTION, I AM HERE REGARDING A CERTAIN MAN CALLED...
TABERNACLE

DEDE.
I KNOW YOU ARE TIRED, BUT THE OTHERS WANT TO MEET YOU
WHAT DO YOU PEOPLE WANT WITH ME?
WE'RE FRIENDS, WE DON'T PLAN TO KILL YOU OR YOU'D BE DEAD, Y'KNOW. *CHUCKLE*
SARCASM! HAHAHA! TO BE ABLE TO MANAGE THAT UNDER THESE CONDITIONS SHOWS INNER STRENGTH; DEFIANCE IS NOT ALWAYS A SIGN OF STUBBORNNESS
HOW COMFORTING! WHERE ARE WE GOING?
WE ARE APPROACHING THE OUTER COURTS, DEDE
THE OUTER COURTS? HMM... THAT SOUNDS VERY CRYPTIC. I DON'T KNOW WHAT YOU GUYS ARE....
WHAT THE...?!!
WHAT IS THE MATTER, DEDE?

YOU THOUGHT YOU SAW?
I THOUGHT I JUST SAW WINGED MEN....ER, WINGED BEINGS GOING UP AND DOWN THAT SMOKE-LIGHT THING!
GROAN FATIGUE IS BEGINNING TO MESS WITH MY MIND. I DREAMT OF MONSTERS WHEN I SLEPT. NOW, I'M SEEING FLYING MEN WHILE AWAKE
HMM... WHY DO YOU THINK THAT IS?
IT MEANS MY MIND IS SO STRESSED, IT'S CREATING IMAGES OF ANGELS AND DEMONS - FAIRYTALE STUFF! IF I DON'T GET AMPLE REST, I'LL SOON START SEEING GOBLINS, ELVES AND SPIDERMAN!
DEDE, I'LL BE BLUNT. YOUR WIFE, ANGELA, DIED FOR REASONS YOU ARE ABOUT TO FIND OUT.
BASICALLY, YOU HAVE WOKEN UP IN THE MIDDLE OF BATTLEFIELD WITH NO FENCE. YOU WILL HAVE TO CHOOSE A SIDE...
YOU WILL HAVE TO BATTLE FORMIDABLE ADVERSARIES.
GENTLEMEN, YOUR LIVES WILL BE ENDING SHORTLY. KINDLY LET ME KNOW IF THERE ARE WORDS OR ITEMS YOU WILL LIKE CONVEYED TO YOUR LOVED ONES?

THE GREATEST EARTHLY WEAPON IS AN ALLOY FORGED WITH TWO PARTS: A HONED MIND AND...
A HONED BODY...
SHOW YOURSELF!!!!
HERE I AM!
flick
HAEEEE!!!
TASH
THE AIR TAKES ON A DIFFERENT QUALITY; MORTAL COMBAT HAS BEGUN.

SO MUCH POWER...SPEED... HOW? HO.....
MOMENTS LATER...
WOOOASSH!!!
IT IS DONE. NOW, CAN I MEET "THE CIRCLE OF SIX"?
LEH-HKAV -AH...
OK. YES.....YES....I ALSO WANT TO KNOW WHAT IS ON THAT USB DRIVE.

OH GOD! I MISSED YOU. I THOUGHT I LOST YOU!
I MISSED YOU, DADDY. I WAS SO SCARED WHEN THE BAD PEOPLE TOOK ME.
DEDE, IF YOU DON'T MIND, I WOULD LIKE TO MAKE THAT HUG SO MUCH BETTER...
YOUR BODY SHOULD BE FINE NOW. YOU CAN LEAVE THE WHEELCHAIR...
WOW! I FEEL NO PAIN! HOW THE HECK DID YOU DO THAT?!
WOW! DADDY, YOU CAN STAND!
WHO ARE YOU GUYS?!

WHO ARE WE? HMM...GOOD QUESTION. WELL, WE ARE WHO WE HOPE YOU WILL BECOME
UHM... WHAT KIND OF ANSWER IS THAT?
A PARTLY CRYPTIC ONE, I SUPPOSE. I HAVE A LOT TO SHOW YOU - BUT THE REAL QUESTION IS, ARE YOU READY TO KNOW THE TRUTH, DEDE?
WELL, YOU REALISE THESE ARE THE KIND OF WORDS YOU HEAR WHEN SOMEONE WANTS TO DRAG YOU INTO SOME DUMB CULT
FAIR POINT. BUT IT'S NOT EVERYDAY A DUMB CULT HEALS YOU INSTANTLY, IN A VERIFIABLE MANNER.
LET ME SIMPLIFY THIS, DEDE...DO YOU WANT TO KNOW WHY YOUR WIFE DIED? WHY SHE WAS KILLED?
I UNDERSTAND HER DEATH BRINGS PAIN. AND ANGER
BUT ON THE BATTLEFIELD, EMOTIONS ARE NOT ENOUGH. CHOICES MUST STILL BE MADE. SO, DO YOU WANT TO KNOW WHY YOUR WIFE WAS KILLED, DEDE?
Y-YES...
THEN, COME WITH ME, DEDE...

THE EPOCH UNIVERSE IN YOUR HANDS

Are you a Kindle user? We are happy to announce that all Epoch Comics titles can now be purchased on the biggest global selling platform for books @Amazon.com. Take advantage of the convenience!

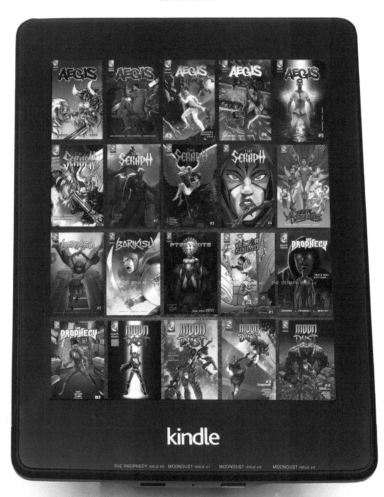

ALL COMICS BY EPOCH
NOW
AVAILABLE ON

DEDE KNOWS ONLY *TWO* THINGS; HE IS NOT MAD - AND YET HIS *LIFE* IS CURRENTLY STRANGER THAN *FICTION*.

IN SUMMARY, HE IS AN *AWARD WINNING* JOURNALIST WHO HAS LOST HIS WIFE OVER A USB STICK AND IS NOW *FLYING* IN OUTER SPACE, *LITERALLY* HELD BY THE STURDY ARMS OF *ANGELS*.

THAT *LOOKS* LIKE A GOOD SPOT FOR OUR *TALK*. WHAT DO YOU THINK, *FOLKS*?

WHAT'S *FUNNY*?

HAHA HA HA HA

WHAT ??!!!

WHAT IS *THIS* PLACE?

I'LL *CLARIFY*. THERE IS A GUARDIAN WATCHER CALLED MOLASH, A DEAR FRIEND OF MINE. RIGHT *NOW*, WE ARE ON HIS *SCALP*.

THE "HAIR OF MOLASH"? ODD NAME FOR A *PLACE*.

THIS IS THE *HAIR OF MOLASH*.

THE *OTHERS* FIND IT *FUNNY* THAT I LIKE THIS SPOT. SO, WE'RE ON THE *HAIR OF MOLASH* AND AROUND US YOU CAN SEE HIS *HAIR FOLLICLES*.

AEGIS
EPISODE 6: ILLUMINATION

FAN
DIMENSION

And so we come to the "end" of the first part of the beginning! It's been quite an interesting journey to see how the story has evolved for Dede who goes from being "naive" to becoming the hunted - and then, in some way, becoming the "hunter". If you think the story has been interesting or intriguing, then think again, because, as they say, "you ain't seen nothing yet!".

There are a lot of plot twists ahead and answers to many questions: Why did his wife have to die, even with so many angels around? What happens to his daughter? Apart from the Presidential candidate, who are the other members of the cult - and what are their intentions? All these and more are answered in the coming episodes of Aegis.

And if you think The Knife is an intriguing villain, then wait until you see... Well, let's just say "her" at this point; less is more. There will be new characters on all sides of the divide and we hope to give you a lot of "aha" moments that will explain parts of the story, and even some complicated questions about life as we know it.

So a big "thank you" to readers and lovers of this series as well as all supporters of the Epoch comic universe. We will do our best to keep churning out beautiful comics that are meaningful, and that are worth your time. And keep your feedback and thoughts coming in; they are genuinely appreciated.

Yours Sincerely

J.C. Nova signing out...

Check us out across the major social media platforms and drop your feedback realtime. Our handles are below.

Enter the Epochverse!

f epochcomics
𝕏 @epochcomics_ng
◎ @epochstudiosng   *FOLLOW US NOW!*

ⓔ epoch **March 2018** all rights reserved

www.epochstudios.co

AEGIS BARASU MANU DUST PROPHECY DINTA SCRIMM PTERYGOTE MALLET TRU ADDA MASTER SQUAD